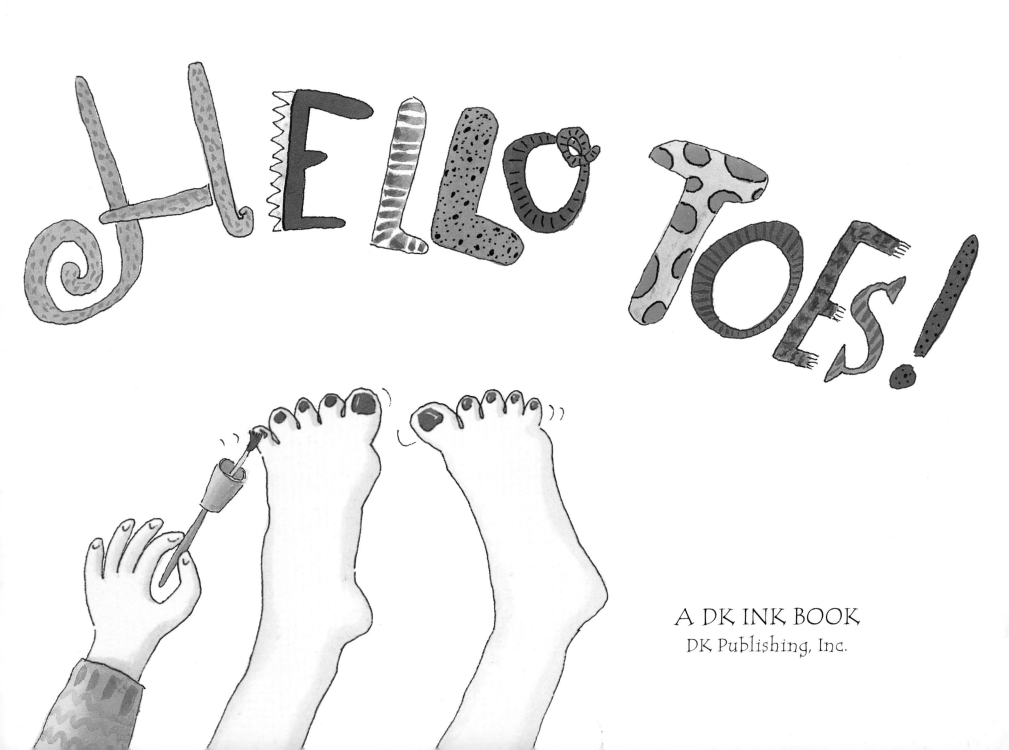

A DK INK BOOK
DK Publishing, Inc.

Hello Feet!

by Ann Whitford Paul

illustrated by Nadine Bernard Westcott

Good morning, toes,

Good morning, feet,

tangled up between
my sheets.

Be the first to touch the floor,

hop me to the closet door.

I've got socks,
I've got shoes,
Let me put them
on for you.

Clump
down the hall,
clomp
down
the
stairs

to the kitchen,
to my chair.
Kick the table
while I eat.

Go outside,
try to leap

across the walk,

skip side to side,

lead the way
quick down
the slide.

I'm swinging now!
Point up high,
see if you can touch the sky.

Hello, toes,
Hello, feet,

jump rock to rock
across the creek.

Rush me home
to get my lunch.

Be cat's paws
that pad the ground,
creeping . . .
S h h h h h h h h h h h !
Don't make a sound.

Be horse's hooves.
Come on!
Let's trot.

Now march me over
to the trees.
Shuffle through the
pile of leaves.

I'll slip off your socks
and shoes.
Squish into the
muddy ooze.

Spin me slow,

spin me fast,

stomp and make the puddle **SPLASH!**

Wiggle lots,
sink down deep.

I'll hose you off,

it's time to eat.

Be the first to touch
my bath,

the last to dry,
and after that,

snuggle in between my sheets.

Good night, toes.

Good night, feet.

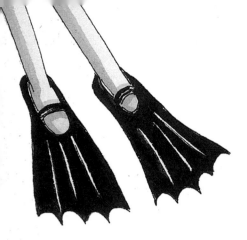

For Rob, Debbie, Dave, and Brad—apart,
but still close   A.W.P.

For Becky   N.B.W.

A Melanie Kroupa Book

DK
Ink

DK Publishing, Inc., 95 Madison Avenue, New York, New York 10016

Visit us on the World Wide Web at http://www.dk.com

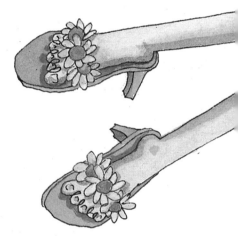

Library of Congress Cataloging-in-Publication Data
Paul, Ann Whitford
   Hello toes! Hello feet! / by Ann Whitford Paul ; illustrated by
Nadine Bernard Westcott — 1st ed.
      p.   cm.
   "A Melanie Kroupa book"
   Summary: A girl takes delight in all the things she and her feet do
throughout the day.
   ISBN 0-7894-2481-9
   [1. Foot—Fiction. 2. Day—Fiction. 3. Stories in rhyme.]
I. Westcott, Nadine Bernard, ill. II. Title.
PZ8.3.P273645Hf   1998   97-31002
[E]—dc21   CIP
                                                         AC

Book design by Chris Hammill Paul
The text of this book is set in 26 point ITC Tempus

Printed and bound in the United States of America
First Edition, 1998

4   6   8   10   9   7   5   3

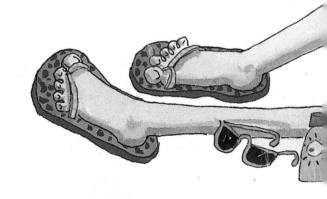